MW01055183

CYNDY SZEKERES'
Favorite Fairy Tales

14 All-Time Classics

Selected and adapted by Selma G. Lanes
Illustrated by Cyndy Szekeres

A GOLDEN BOOK • NEW YORK
Western Publishing Company, Inc., Racine, Wisconsin 53404

© 1988, 1983 Western Publishing Company, Inc. Illustrations © 1991, 1988, 1983 Cyndy Szekeres. All rights reserved. Printed in the U.S.A. No part of this book may be reproduced or copied in any form without written permission from the publisher. All trademarks are the property of Western Publishing Company, Inc. Library of Congress Catalog Card Number: 91-71219 ISBN 0-307-15507-2/ISBN: 0-307-67507-6 (lib. bdg.)   MCMXCII

Originally published in two volumes as
Cyndy Szekeres' Book of Nursery Tales and *Cyndy Szekeres' Book of Fairy Tales*

Table of Contents

The Three Bears

Once upon a time, there were three bears: a Great Big Bear, a Middle-sized Bear, and a Wee Small Bear. They lived deep in the forest in a house all their own.

Every morning the three bears cooked hot porridge for their breakfast. While the porridge cooled, they went out for a walk.

One day a little girl named Goldilocks, who lived on the far side of the forest, came upon their house and peeked inside.

Seeing nobody home, she tried the door. It wasn't locked, so Goldilocks went inside.

She was hungry, and when she saw three bowls of porridge on the kitchen table, Goldilocks was as happy as she could be. First she tasted the porridge in the Great Big Bowl, but it was too hot. Next she tasted the porridge in the Middle-sized Bowl, but it was too cold. Then she tasted the porridge in the Wee Small Bowl—and it was just right. So she ate it all up.

Goldilocks had walked a long way and felt tired. When she saw three chairs in the next room, she was as happy as she could be. First she tried the Great Big Chair, but it was too hard. Next she tried the Middle-sized Chair, but it was too soft. Then she tried the Wee Small Chair—and it felt just right. But Goldilocks was too heavy for it, and the chair broke all to pieces.

Feeling sleepy, Goldilocks went into the bedroom. There she found three beds side by side, and she was as happy as she could be. First she tried the Great Big Bed, but it was too hard. Next she tried the Middle-sized Bed, but it was too soft. Then she tried the Wee Small Bed—and it was just right. So she fell fast asleep.

Now the three bears came home to eat their breakfast. When the Great Big Bear found a spoon in his porridge, he roared in his Great Big Voice, **"SOMEBODY HAS BEEN EATING MY PORRIDGE!"**

Then the Middle-sized Bear saw a spoon in her porridge, and she cried out in her Middle-sized Voice, "SOMEBODY HAS BEEN EATING MY PORRIDGE!"

When the Wee Small Bear looked at his empty bowl, he squeaked in his Wee Small Voice, "SOMEBODY HAS BEEN EATING MY PORRIDGE—AND IT'S ALL GONE!"

So the three bears began to look about. When the Great Big Bear
looked at his armchair, he found the cushion out of place. He roared in
his Great Big Voice, **"SOMEBODY HAS BEEN SITTING IN MY
CHAIR!"**

When the Middle-sized Bear looked at her armchair, she found the
pillow on the floor. So she complained in her Middle-sized Voice,
"SOMEBODY HAS BEEN SITTING IN MY CHAIR!"

Then the Wee Small Bear looked at his chair and cried out,
"SOMEBODY HAS BEEN SITTING IN MY CHAIR—AND IT'S BROKEN ALL
TO PIECES!"

Next the three bears went into the bedroom. When the Great Big Bear found his bolster out of place, he roared in his Great Big Voice, **"SOMEBODY HAS BEEN LYING IN MY BED!"**

When the Middle-sized Bear found her blankets mussed, she said in her Middle-sized Voice, "SOMEBODY HAS BEEN LYING IN MY BED!"

Then the Wee Small Bear looked at his bed and cried out, "SOMEBODY HAS BEEN LYING IN MY BED—AND HERE SHE IS!"

So shrill was the voice of the Wee Small Bear that Goldilocks awoke at once. When she saw the three bears looking at her, she was as frightened as she could be. She leapt out of the bed, jumped through the low, open window, and ran home as fast as her legs could carry her.

The three bears never ever saw Goldilocks again.

The Elves and the Shoemaker

Once upon a time, there lived a shoemaker. Though he worked very hard, he was so poor that at last he had enough leather left for only one pair of shoes.

On a winter's night he cut out the shoes, but he was too tired and discouraged to finish them. He left the leather on his workbench and went to bed.

The shoemaker had no idea what he and his wife would do now that all the leather was used up. There was no money to buy more. But despite their troubles, the shoemaker and his wife slept soundly.

Early next morning the shoemaker awoke and dressed. Then he went into his shop to make the last pair of shoes.

He sat down at his bench and picked up his hammer. But what was this?!! The shoemaker thought he must be dreaming, but it was no dream. On the very spot where he had left the leather the night before, there lay a finished pair of beautiful shoes.

He called his wife to show her the shoes. "How splendid!" she exclaimed. "When did you make them?"

"I didn't make them," the shoemaker replied. "I found them here this morning!"

No sooner had the shoemaker put the shoes in his window than the door of his shop swung open and a fine gentleman walked inside.

"I must have those wonderful shoes," he said. "The stitches are so small and delicate! I've never seen any like them."

The shoemaker happily sold the shoes to the gentleman for a very high price.

With the money the shoemaker bought leather for two pairs of shoes. Enough money was left over to buy a soup bone for dinner.

That night he cut out the leather, but he was very hungry. He could smell the soup his wife was cooking. "I'll make the shoes tomorrow," he said and went to eat his dinner.

Next morning he found two pairs of elegant shoes on his workbench! Again he showed them to his wife. "Who can be making these marvelous shoes?" she wondered.

The shoemaker wondered, too. Once again, no sooner had he placed the shoes in his window than the shop door swung open. This time there were two customers, and they both paid the shoemaker handsomely for the shoes.

Now he had money enough to buy leather for four pairs of shoes.

Things went on in this way for some time. Each night the shoemaker cut the leather and went to sleep. And each morning he found more beautiful shoes on his workbench!

The shoemaker was becoming rich.

One evening he said to his wife, "It's nearly Christmas, and still we don't know who is making the shoes. We cannot go another day without finding out who is helping us."

So, instead of going to sleep that night, the shoemaker and his wife hid in the shop.

At midnight two tiny elves tiptoed into the room. The shoemaker and his wife watched in amazement as the elves busily stitched and sewed and hammered.

Soon the bench was filled with beautiful new shoes. The moment their work was finished the elves vanished.

"Incredible!" the shoemaker cried. "We must do something for these tiny creatures who have been so kind."

"Well," said his wife, "the poor little things had neither clothes nor shoes on, and they must get very cold this time of year."

So the shoemaker's wife made two tiny suits for the elves. And the shoemaker fashioned two perfect pairs of tiny shoes.

The following night they laid the things they had made on the bench and once again hid behind the curtain.

At midnight the elves came into the room. When they saw the outfits, they were overjoyed. They tried them on, and they fitted just right.

The elves danced round and round the room and sang a merry song.

At last they danced right out the door, never to return.

But the shoemaker and his wife, who had repaid kindness with kindness, never wanted for anything ever again. What's more, they lived happily—and prosperously—for a good long time.

The Emperor's New Clothes

Once upon a time, there lived an emperor who was fond of beautiful clothes. One day two swindlers came to the palace where he lived. Pretending to be weavers, they told the emperor about a most wonderful cloth they could make. Not only was it incredibly beautiful, but it possessed a magical quality: It could not be seen by anyone who was stupid.

"I should like to have clothes made of this magic material," the emperor thought. "Then I could tell the clever from the stupid in my kingdom." So he ordered a suit from the two impostors and gave them the large sum of money they demanded in advance.

At once the tricksters set to work. They set up their looms and asked for only the finest silks and the most beautiful gold thread to use in weaving their cloth. They hid these costly materials in their traveling bags and pretended to be hard at work on the bare looms.

"I wonder how the weavers are coming along with the cloth for my new suit," the emperor thought after a few days. "I'll send my wise old prime minister to find out. He will tell me if the fabric is all they promise."

So the prime minister went to the room where the impostors sat at their bare looms. "Goodness gracious!" the prime minister said to himself. Though his eyes were wide open, he could not see any cloth at all.

Both swindlers asked how he liked their work. Had he ever seen cloth of so brilliant a color? Or with so elegant a pattern? The poor prime minister opened his eyes wider still. "Can it be," he thought, "that I am stupid? No one must find out!

"It is very pretty! Quite dazzling, in fact!" the old minister said aloud, squinting over his spectacles. "I shall tell the emperor at once." And he did, much to the emperor's delight.

Now the scoundrels demanded more money, more silk, and more gold thread, all of which they put into their traveling bags. Not a single strand of thread was put upon the looms, though the impostors continued to pretend they were weaving.

Again the emperor grew impatient. This time he sent the grand duke to find out when the wondrous cloth would be ready. Once more the swindlers displayed their empty looms. Was the cloth not superb, its pattern incredible? The poor grand duke looked and looked, but he saw nothing whatsoever.

"If I am stupid," the grand duke thought in panic, "the secret must rest with me!" So he praised the cloth enthusiastically. "It is lovely beyond words," he told the emperor on his return.

By now, everyone in the city was talking about the weavers and their magnificent cloth.

At last the emperor wanted to see the fabulous fabric for himself. With all his courtiers he marched to the workroom of the two impostors. As usual, the swindlers were busily at work, though the emperor could see nothing on their looms.

"Isn't the cloth magnificent?" the weavers simpered. "Your Majesty must look closely. Examine the intricate design and the beauty of the colors."

"My word!" the emperor thought. "I see absolutely nothing. Can it be that I am stupid?"

"It is the most beautiful cloth I have ever seen," the emperor said aloud. "I approve most heartily."

His courtiers all hastened to agree. Of course, they saw no more than the emperor had seen, but they did not wish to be thought stupid. They urged the emperor to be fitted for a suit at once. Perhaps he could wear it in the grand procession the very next day.

The imposters agreed to stay up all night to finish the suit. They pretended to take the cloth off the loom and to cut it and sew it as well. Everyone could see how busy they were. At last they announced, "The emperor's new clothes are ready!"

Both swindlers then pretended to hold things up for the emperor to try on. "Here are the trousers," they said. "Next comes the jacket. And last of all the cloak.

"The cloth is so light in weight," they told the emperor slyly, "that you may feel as though you are wearing nothing."

The imposters then pretended to help their foolish customer try on his new garments. The emperor did as he was told.

"How beautifully my new suit fits!" the emperor said nervously. "The design and color are perfect."

A servant entered to announce that the procession was about to begin.

"Well, I am ready," the emperor said. "My outfit is magnificent!"

His pages stooped and pretended to pick up the end of the emperor's long cloak. They dared not confess that they, too, saw nothing at all.

So the emperor walked proudly in the procession, under a magnificent canopy.

The people in the street, and those watching from the windows, all said, "The emperor's suit is stupendous!" No one dared to admit that he saw nothing, for that would mean he was stupid.

Just one little child blurted out the truth, "Why, the emperor is wearing no clothes at all!"

A few people laughed when they heard this. Others whispered nervously. Then everyone looked at the emperor again.

"The child is right!" people said at last. "The emperor is wearing no clothes at all."

Then the emperor knew this was true. But he said to himself, "In any case, I must go on with the procession." And so the poor emperor kept on walking till he got home and could put on some real clothes that he and everyone else could see.

Stone Soup

Once upon a time, a small child saw three wayfarers strolling down the road into town. "Strangers are coming!" he cried, running through the streets.

Now the townspeople had just harvested their crops and were busy storing food for the winter.

"Strangers coming here?" said one. "They'll have traveled a long way and are bound to be hungry."

"After all our hard work, they'll want us to share our food with them," said another.

"Let's hurry and hide it," said a third. "Then we can tell them we have none to share."

All through the town, people hid their food down in cellars, up in attics, under floors, and behind doors. Then they shut themselves in their houses and closed the curtains so the strangers would see that they did not wish to be disturbed.

The three wayfarers were just poor fellows trying to make their way in the world. When they reached the town, they were hungry and tired.

"How I would like a bowl of hot soup!" said one.

"Me too," said the second.

"Let's ask the good people of this town if they will give us some soup," said the third.

So the three friends went up to a house and knocked long and hard. After a while, the door opened a crack.

"We are three weary wanderers," said the first traveler. "Can you spare a bowl of soup for us?"

"No soup here," answered a voice from inside the house. "There's no food at all in this poor town. You'd best be on your way." And the door slammed shut.

The wayfarers tried other houses with no better luck. At last one of them had an idea.

"The fields and gardens in this town have been picked clean," he said. "There must be food here, if only we could get some. We shall have to make stone soup.

"Ask to borrow a kettle at that house," he told one friend. "Try to get some wood for kindling at the next," he told the other. "I will gather three good round stones."

At the first house one wayfarer said, "Since you have no food, may we borrow a kettle for cooking stone soup?"

"Stone soup?" asked the townsman. "How do you make that?"

"Lend your kettle and you will see," said the wayfarer. "We'll give you a taste when it's done."

"Is stone soup good?" asked the townsman.

"More delicious than you can imagine," said the wayfarer.

He got the kettle, and his friend got some kindling after praising the wonders of stone soup. Then they set about borrowing matches and buckets of water, all the while boasting of the tastiness of stone soup.

By the time they returned to the square with what they had gathered, everyone was curious about stone soup. The townspeople all watched to see what the wayfarers would do.

They built a fire and set the kettle filled with water over it. When the water was boiling, they carefully plopped the three round stones into the pot, one by one. Then they sat down, as if waiting for the soup to cook.

"That's no way to make a soup," said one townsman. "Surely stone soup needs carrots. And, well—I guess I can spare some carrots myself." He ran down to his cellar and brought out a big bunch of carrots to the wayfarers in the square.

"Thank you," said one stranger. "Nothing's as good as stone soup with carrots." He cut them up and dropped them into the kettle.

"Carrots indeed!" muttered a woman watching from her window. "What that soup needs is onions." From under her floor she lifted a large bag of onions and dragged it into the square.

"Ah, nothing's as good as stone soup with onions," said another wayfarer, starting to peel them. "Thank you, dear madam!"

And so it went. Beets and parsnips, celery and potatoes, barley and peas were all added to the stone soup. Soon everyone in town had brought something tasty for the pot. The wayfarers kept stirring, and the aroma of a delicious soup filled the air.

At long last, when everyone had had a taste, they all agreed that nothing in the whole wide world is as good as stone soup.

The Three Little Pigs

Once upon a time, there were three little pigs who went out into the world to seek their fortunes.

The first little pig met a man with a bundle of straw. "Please, sir," he said, "will you give me some straw to build myself a house?"

The man did, and the little pig built himself a house of straw.

By and by, along came a wolf who knocked at the door and said, "LITTLE PIG, LITTLE PIG, LET ME COME IN!"

To which the pig answered, "Not by the hair of my chinny-chin-chin."

This made the wolf angry, and he said, "Then I'll huff and I'll puff and I'll blow your house in!"

So he huffed and he puffed and he blew the house in, and he ate up the first little pig.

The second little pig met a man with a stack of wood. "Please, sir," he said, "will you give me some wood to build myself a house?"

The man did, and the little pig built himself a house of wood.

By and by, along came the wolf, who knocked at the door and said, "LITTLE PIG, LITTLE PIG, LET ME COME IN!"

To which the pig answered, "Not by the hair of my chinny-chin-chin."

"Then I'll huff and I'll puff and I'll blow your house in!" snarled the wolf.

Well, he huffed and he puffed, and he puffed and he huffed, and he blew the house in. Then he ate up the second little pig.

The third little pig met a man with a load of bricks. "Please, sir," he said, "will you give me some bricks to build myself a house?"

The man did, and the little pig built himself a house of bricks.

By and by, along came the wolf, who knocked at the door and said, "LITTLE PIG, LITTLE PIG, LET ME COME IN!"

"Not by the hair of my chinny-chin-chin," said the third little pig.

"Then I'll huff and I'll puff and I'll blow your house in!"

Well, that wolf, he huffed and he puffed, and he puffed and he huffed, and he huffed and he puffed some more. But he could not blow the brick house in.

So the sly wolf said, "Little pig, I know where there is a field full of sweet turnips."

"Where?" asked the little pig.

"At Farmer Smith's. If you'll be ready tomorrow morning at six o'clock, we can go together and get some for dinner."

Next morning, the little pig got up at five o'clock and was back home with sweet turnips for his dinner before the wolf even came by.

When the wolf discovered that he had been tricked, he was angrier than ever. Still, he said in a friendly way, "Little pig, I know where there is a tree full of ripe red apples."

"Where?" asked the little pig.

"Down at Merry Garden. Tomorrow morning I will come by at five o'clock, and we can go pick some together."

This time the pig got up at four o'clock and had picked almost a basketful of ripe red apples when he saw the wolf coming. The little pig was frightened.

"What, here already?" said the wolf, licking his chops. "Are the apples tasty?"

"Delicious!" said the little pig. "Try one." And he threw an apple so far that, while the wolf chased after it, the pig was able to jump down from the tree and run home.

The wolf howled with rage.

But, next day, he came again and said, "Little pig, there is a fair at Shanklin this afternoon. Let's go together at three o'clock."

At one o'clock the little pig ran off to the fair, where he bought himself a big wooden butter churn. He was carrying it home when suddenly he saw the wolf coming. Quick as a wink, the pig jumped inside the churn to hide. By accident, he turned it over, and, bumpety-bump, the churn rolled down the hill right toward the wolf.

The wolf was so frightened by the strange object that he ran home without even going to the fair.

Later he went by the pig's house to tell him about the scary thing that had chased him down the hill.

The little pig laughed. "That was the butter churn I bought at the fair," he said, "with me inside it."

The wolf was so angry that he decided to eat up the little pig right then and there. "I will go down the chimney," he said to himself. But the little pig heard the wolf clumping up onto his roof and hung a pot full of water in the fireplace. Then he lit a blazing fire beneath it.

As the wolf started down the chimney, the pig lifted the cover of the pot. *Plop!* The wolf fell into the boiling water, and that was the end of him. As for the little pig, he didn't miss the wicked wolf one bit.

The Little Red Hen

Once upon a time, a little red hen was scratching in the barnyard and found some grains of wheat.

"This wheat should be planted," said she. "Who will plant these grains of wheat?"

"Not I," said the Duck.

"Not I," said the Lamb.

"Not I," said the Dog.

"Then I will," said the Little Red Hen. And she did.

When the wheat grew tall and yellow, the Little Red Hen said, "This wheat is ready to harvest. Who will cut the wheat?"

"Not I," said the Duck.

"Not I," said the Lamb.

"Not I," said the Dog.

"Then I will," said the Little Red Hen. And she did.

When the wheat was cut, the Little Red Hen said, "Now the seeds must be separated from the stems. Who will thresh the wheat?"

"Not I," said the Duck.

"Not I," said the Lamb.

"Not I," said the Dog.

"Then I will," said the Little Red Hen. And she did.

When the wheat was threshed, the Little Red Hen said, "This wheat should be ground into flour. Who will take this wheat to the miller?"

"Not I," said the Duck.

"Not I," said the Lamb.

"Not I," said the Dog.

"Then I will," said the Little Red Hen. And she did.

After the wheat was ground into flour, the Little Red Hen said, "This flour should be made into dough and baked into bread. Who will bake the bread?"

"Not I," said the Duck.

"Not I," said the Lamb.

"Not I," said the Dog.

"Then I will," said the Little Red Hen. And she did.

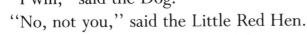

When the bread was baked, the Little Red Hen said, "This warm bread should be eaten. Who will eat this bread?"

"I will," said the Duck.

"I will," said the Lamb.

"I will," said the Dog.

"No, not you," said the Little Red Hen. "I will eat this bread." And she did.

The Two Frogs

Once upon a time, there were two frogs. One lived in a mud hole near the port city of Southampton, England. The other lived in a clear pond in the capital city of London.

The two frogs lived far apart, and neither knew that the other existed. Yet, one morning, each had the very same thought—to see something of the great wide world.

So, on the same day, both started out from opposite ends of the long road connecting Southampton and London.

"Hip, hop. Hippety-hop," croaked the Southampton frog. "I'll hop right to London before I stop."

"Hop, hip. Hoppety-hip," croaked the London frog. "I'll reach Southampton my very first trip."

The way was longer and harder than either frog had expected. On and on they hopped. Hop, hip, hoppety-hip. Hip, hop, hippety-hop.

At last they came to opposite sides of the very same high hill. "Hip, hop," croaked each frog wearily. "I'll have to reach that mountaintop." It took them one thousand hops each to get to the top. The frogs were astonished to see one another.

"Hello, there!" said the Southampton frog. "Where do you come from and where are you going?"

"Hello to you!" replied the London frog. "I come from the capital city and am on my way to visit Southampton."

"What a coincidence!" said the first frog. "I come from that port city and am on my way to see London!"

They sat down to rest. "It's a tiring trip," said the Southampton frog with a sigh. "If I could just catch sight of where I am going, the rest of the journey might seem easier."

"If only we were taller," said the London frog, "we might be able to see both cities from this high mountain."

"We could make ourselves taller," said the Southampton frog, "by standing on our hind legs and holding on to each other's shoulders for balance. Then we could lift our heads way up and see the cities we are traveling to."

So the London frog and the Southampton frog jumped up on their hind legs and held on to each other's shoulders. The Southampton frog was facing toward London, and the London frog toward Southampton. However, the foolish creatures forgot that, in this strange position, their great, bulgy eyes would see backward instead of forward. Although their bodies faced the cities to which they were traveling, their pop-eyes looked right back at the cities from which they had come.

"Amazing!" cried the Southampton frog. "London looks exactly like Southampton. It is hardly worth the bother to visit."

"Incredible!" said the London frog. "Southampton is the twin of London. I may just as well go home."

So both frogs turned around and hopped back to their own cities. Hippety-hop, hoppety-hip. And they lived happily ever after, each believing that the port city of Southampton and the capital city of London—which are very different places indeed—were as alike as two lily pads in a frog pond.

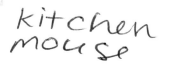
kitchen
mouse

The Three Little Kittens

Once upon a time, there were three little kittens who lived with their mother in a snug little cottage.

When winter came with its cold and snow, Mother Cat knitted three pairs of mittens. She wanted the three little kittens' paws to stay warm.

The first pair of mittens was bright red. The second pair was pale green, and the third was deep blue. The three little kittens put on their mittens and ran outside to play.

"Be good little kittens. Don't lose your mittens!" called Mother Cat. "I shall bake a pie."

First the three little kittens threw snowballs. Next they rolled a big snowcat, and then they made kitten angels by falling backward into the soft white snow.

The first little kitten had very wet mittens, so he took them off and hung them on a branch to dry.

The second little kitten saw a feather in the snow and pulled off his mittens to pick it up.

The third little kitten needed her sharp claws to climb a tree and chase a bird, so she dropped her mittens by the tree trunk.

The bird flew away, but the kitten in the tree looked all around at the world beneath her. In the distance she saw a big brown dog. The dog was heading toward the three of them! The kitten scrambled down the tree to warn her brothers, and the three little kittens ran lickety-split home.

Mother Cat was waiting. "Just in time for warm pie and milk, my pets," she said. Then she saw that the three little kittens had no mittens. The kittens looked at their paws.

The three little kittens,
  They lost their mittens,
And they began to cry,
  "Oh Mommy dear,
  We sadly fear
  Our mittens we have lost!"

"What! Lost your mittens?
  You naughty kittens!
  Then you shall have no pie."

  Miew, miew. Miew, miew.
"No, you shall have no pie."

The three little kittens went to look for their mittens. They hunted high and low. The first little kitten saw his red mittens hanging on the branch. The second little kitten found his green mittens half buried in the snow. The third little kitten spied her blue mittens lying at the bottom of the tree.

The three little kittens,
They found their mittens,
And they began to shout,
"Oh Mommy dear,
See here! See here!
Our mittens we have found."

"What! Found your mittens?
You darling kittens!
Then you shall have some pie."

Purr, purr. Purr, purr.
"Yes, you shall have some pie."

So the three little kittens sat down to eat delicious slices of apple pie. But they were so hungry that they forgot to take off their mittens!

The three little kittens,
They wore their mittens,
And soon ate up the pie.
"Oh Mommy dear,
We greatly fear
Our mittens we have soiled."

"What! Soiled your mittens?
You careless kittens!"
Then they began to sigh.

Miew, miew. Miew, miew.
Yes, they began to sigh.

The three little kittens filled the washtub with soapy water. Then they rubbed their mittens and scrubbed their mittens until they were as clean as clean could be.

The three little kittens,
 They washed their mittens,
And hung them up to dry.
 "Oh Mommy dear,
 Look here! Look here!
 Our mittens we have washed."

"What! Washed your mittens?
 You helpful kittens.
But I smell a rat close by."

Miew, miew. Hush! Hush!
"I smell a rat close by."

For the rest of the winter, right up to the first warm day of spring, the three little kittens took good care of their mittens. They didn't lose them or soil them again. Purr, purr. Purr, purr.

The Brementown Musicians

Once upon a time, there was a donkey who lived on a farm. He earned his daily oats and hay by carting sacks of wheat from the fields to the mill, where it was ground into flour. When, at last, the donkey grew too old and weary for such work, he decided to leave the farm and go to live in the nearby town of Bremen. He thought he might become a street musician there and entertain the townspeople with old songs. He would use the coins they tossed to him for food and lodging.

He had not traveled far when he met a dog lying by the side of the road. "How now, my friend?" inquired the donkey.

"I am running away," the dog replied. "I have grown too old to hunt, and I want to try something new."

"Then why not come with me?" asked the donkey. "I am going to try my luck as a street musician in Bremen. Dogs have powerful voices, so perhaps you can do the same."

The dog liked the idea. "But I'm far too tired to walk all the way to Bremen," he said with a sigh.

"Hop onto my back," the donkey offered, "and we can practice our singing as we go along."

Each time the donkey brayed, "Hee, haw! Hee, hee, haw!" the dog would bark, "Bow, wow! Bow, wow, wow!"

Soon they met a sad and sorry cat. The frown on her face was as long as a lonesome road in winter.

"What is the matter, dear puss?" inquired the donkey.

"I am getting old," the cat replied, "and I can no longer catch mice. I am running away to try something new, but I really don't know what to do."

"Everyone knows cats are good at serenading," said the donkey. "Come with us to Bremen. I am sure you can become a musician there."

The cat happily agreed. She hopped onto the dog's back and joined her new companions in practicing their music. The donkey brayed, "Hee, haw! Hee, hee, haw!" The dog barked, "Bow, wow! Bow, wow, wow!" And the cat caterwauled, "Mew, mew, meoooOOW!"

After traveling some distance, the three friends came to a barnyard. On the gatepost a woebegone rooster perched, his head hanging low.

"What makes you so sad, noble fowl?" inquired the donkey.

"Alas, I am getting too old to greet the dawn," replied the rooster, "but I still have plenty of song left in me. I heard your music in the distance, and I should like to join in."

"Well," said the donkey, "we are on our way to Bremen to become town musicians. Since you have such a fine loud voice, why not come along?"

The rooster readily accepted the invitation. He hopped onto the cat's head, and they all practiced in harmony. The donkey brayed, "Hee, haw! Hee, hee, haw!" The dog barked, "Bow, wow! Bow, wow, wow!" The cat caterwauled, "Mew, mew, meoooOOW!" And the rooster crowed, "Cock-a-doodle-de-doo!"

Since they could not reach Bremen in one day, the four companions decided to spend the night in the woods.

The donkey and the dog lay down under a large tree. The cat nestled beside them, and the rooster flew up to the very treetop.

Before they fell asleep, the rooster noticed a light in the distance. "There must be a house over there," he said.

"Let us go and look," said the donkey. "There may be shelter and food for us." The dog hopped onto the donkey's back, the cat climbed up on the dog's back, and the rooster perched on the donkey's head.

The donkey carried his friends toward the light. It was coming from a lamp inside a cozy little cottage. The donkey stopped at the window. The friends all peered inside.

They saw a big pot filled with food and a group of raccoons eating greedily. Sacks of grain lay all about the room.

"Robbers, by the look of them," whispered the dog.

"If only we could get inside," said the donkey. "It looks so warm and cozy."

"And just see that vegetable stew!" exclaimed the cat.

"Yum!" said the rooster.

"I am starving!" the dog said, drooling.

"Maybe they would give us some of their supper if they liked our singing," said the donkey. Standing by the windowsill, the four companions began their song. The donkey brayed, "Hee, haw! Hee, hee, haw!" The dog barked, "Bow, wow! Bow, wow, wow!" The cat caterwauled, "Mew, mew, meoooOOW!" And the rooster crowed, "Cock-a-doodle-de-doo!" The window rattled with their commotion.

The robbers fled in terror.

"They must have liked our music," said the delighted donkey. "See all the good food they left for us."

The musicians went inside and ate their fill.

When they had finished eating, each found a comfortable sleeping place. The donkey lay down in the middle of the floor, the dog crouched behind the door, the cat curled up on the hearth, and the rooster perched under the eaves. Soon they fell fast asleep.

From a distance, the robbers were watching the house. It had begun to rain, and they were getting soaked.

"Perhaps we should not have run away," said one robber. "I will go back quietly and see if it is safe for us to return."

Cautiously, the robber crept back and opened the cottage door. In the darkness the cat's fiery eyes looked like burning coals. As the robber approached she leapt up and hissed at him.

When the startled raccoon rushed back toward the door, he bumped into the donkey, who brayed and stamped. Then the dog sprang up and barked.

All the while the rooster crowed "Cock-a-doodle-de-doo!" with all his might.

The terrified robber ran back to his companions as fast as his legs could carry him.

"There are wild things in that house!" he told them. "One flew at me and hissed. Then another growled by the door. And a great monster screamed and pounded the earth, while up above sat a ghost who cried, 'Catch the scoundrel, do!'"

The frightened robbers ran away, never to return.

Now it so happened that the cottage belonged to a farmer who had long tried to get rid of the robbers who stole from him. When he passed by in the morning, he heard the musicians practicing. The farmer peered through the window and saw the four friends sitting around the table, enjoying themselves. The donkey brayed, "Hee-haw! Hee, hee, haw!" The dog barked, "Bow, wow! Bow, wow, wow!" The cat caterwauled, "Mew, mew, meoooOOW!" And the rooster crowed, "Cock-a-doodle-de-doo!"

"That noise will surely keep the robbers away," the farmer thought to himself. "Stay here as long as you like," he called to the four musicians. "I'm getting too old to chase robbers."

As for the donkey, the dog, the cat, and the rooster, they loved their new home. And there they remain to this very day, making music to their hearts' content.

Chicken Little

Once upon a time, Chicken Little was pecking at some corn in the barnyard when—*whack!*—an acorn fell on her head.

"Goodness gracious!" thought Chicken Little. "The sky is falling down. I must run and tell the king."

So Chicken Little went along and went along until she met Henny Penny. "Where are you rushing?" clucked Henny Penny.

"Oh! I'm running to tell the king that the sky is falling down," peeped Chicken Little.

"Dear me!" said Henny Penny. "May I come, too?" So Henny Penny and Chicken Little ran to tell the king the sky was falling down.

They went along and went along until they met Cocky Locky. "Where are you two rushing?" crowed Cocky Locky.

"Oh! We're running to tell the king that the sky is falling down," said Chicken Little and Henny Penny.

"My, oh my!" said Cocky Locky. "May I come, too?" So Cocky Locky, Henny Penny, and Chicken Little ran to tell the king the sky was falling down.

They went along and went along until they met Ducky Daddles. "Where are you three rushing?" quacked Ducky Daddles.

"Oh! We're running to tell the king that the sky is falling down," said Chicken Little, Henny Penny, and Cocky Locky.

"Great heavens!" said Ducky Daddles. "May I come, too?" So Ducky Daddles, Cocky Locky, Henny Penny, and Chicken Little ran to tell the king the sky was falling down.

They went along and went along until they met Goosey Poosey. "Where are you four rushing?" honked Goosey Poosey.

"Oh! We're running to tell the king that the sky is falling down," said Chicken Little, Henny Penny, Cocky Locky, and Ducky Daddles.

"For goodness sakes!" said Goosey Poosey. "May I come, too?" So Goosey Poosey, Ducky Daddles, Cocky Locky, Henny Penny, and Chicken Little ran to tell the king the sky was falling down.

They went along and went along until they met Turkey Lurkey. "Where are you five rushing?" gobbled Turkey Lurkey.

"Oh! We're running to tell the king that the sky is falling down," said Chicken Little, Henny Penny, Cocky Locky, Ducky Daddles, and Goosey Poosey.

"Dreadful!" said Turkey Lurkey. "May I come, too?" So Turkey Lurkey, Goosey Poosey, Ducky Daddles, Cocky Locky, Henny Penny, and Chicken Little ran to tell the king the sky was falling down.

They went along and went along until they met Foxy Woxy. "Where are you six rushing?" barked Foxy Woxy.

"Oh! We're running to tell the king that the sky is falling down," said Chicken Little, Henny Penny, Cocky Locky, Ducky Daddles, Goosey Poosey, and Turkey Lurkey.

"Why didn't you come straight to me?" said Foxy Woxy. "I know a shortcut to the king's palace. Just follow me."

"Oh, yes, most certainly," said Chicken Little, Henny Penny, Cocky Locky, Ducky Daddles, Goosey Poosey, and Turkey Lurkey.

So Turkey Lurkey, Goosey Poosey, Ducky Daddles, Cocky Locky, Henny Penny, and Chicken Little all followed Foxy Woxy.

They went along and went along until they came to a narrow, dark hole. Now this was the door to Foxy Woxy's den. But Foxy Woxy said, "Here we are. The best shortcut to the king's palace. Just follow me."

"Oh, yes, most certainly, right away," said Chicken Little, Henny Penny, Cocky Locky, Ducky Daddles, Goosey Poosey, and Turkey Lurkey.

So Foxy Woxy ran into his den, but he didn't go far. He turned and waited in the dark for the others. First Turkey Lurkey appeared. *Whump!* Foxy Woxy knocked Turkey Lurkey on the head and threw him over his shoulder to roast for supper. Next came Goosey Poosey. *Thump!* Down she went, and Foxy Woxy threw her over his shoulder. So it went with Ducky Daddles and Cocky Locky. But before Foxy Woxy could reach Henny Penny, she cried out a warning to Chicken Little.

So Chicken Little turned her tail feathers and ran back to the barnyard as fast as her legs could carry her. She was so glad to be home that she never again tried to tell the king anything at all.

65

The Princess and the Pea

Once upon a time, there lived a prince who wished to marry a real princess, and so he traveled round the world to find one. He met many young women who claimed to be princesses, but how could he be sure that this was true? Sad to say, he returned to the palace alone.

Then, one stormy night, when claps of thunder shook the walls and rain spilled from the sky like a waterfall, the palace gate bell began to clang. The old king himself went to see who might be there. The queen and prince followed close behind. Before them stood a beautiful princess, but what a state she was in! The rain had drenched her clothing. Even her crown was dripping. The king beckoned her to come inside.

"Who are you, my dear?" he asked.

"A princess," said the princess.

"A real princess?" asked the prince.

"Most definitely," the princess replied.

"Well, we'll soon find out!" the old queen thought. Then she marched into the bedroom where the princess was to sleep that night. She took all the blankets off the bed. Next she lifted the mattress and placed on the bedstead a single small pea.

Then the queen cried out, "More mattresses!"

Chambermaids struggled in with every spare mattress they could find. They piled them higher and higher on the bed.

When, at last, the bed could hold no more, the queen said, "That will do. Now summon the princess. It is time for bed."

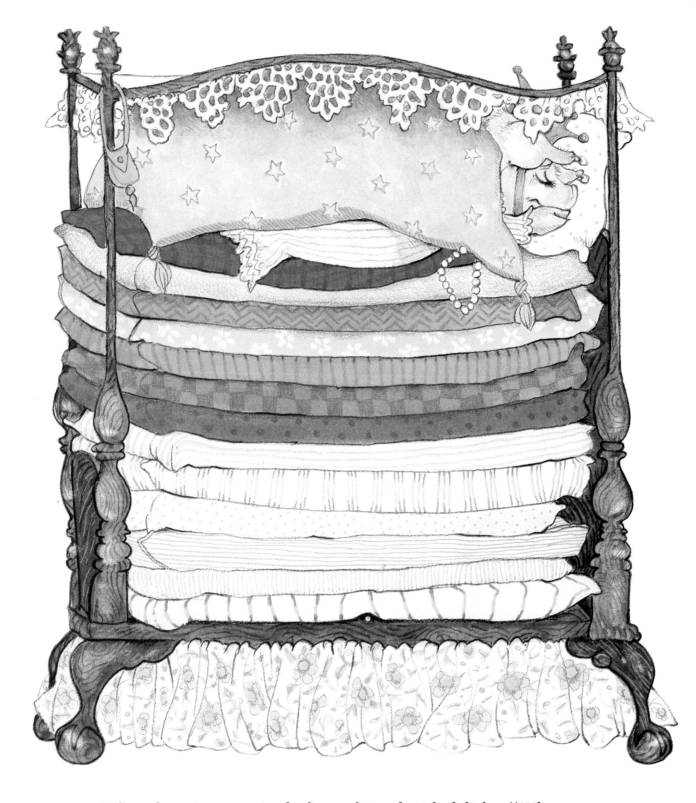

When the princess arrived, she exclaimed with delight, "What a lovely bed! It is surely fit for a princess. I thank you!"

Of course, she needed a ladder to climb into the bed, but soon she settled herself under a fine goose-feather quilt covered with pale blue silk and embroidered with stars. In the blink of an eye, she fell fast asleep.

Then everyone in the castle went to bed, too.

Next morning the queen again marched into the princess's bedroom to ask how she had slept.

"I scarcely closed my eyes the whole night long," the princess answered with a yawn. "Something lumpy and hard was in my bed. I couldn't stop tossing and turning."

Overjoyed, the queen called for the prince. "This is, indeed, a real princess," she declared. "Through thirteen mattresses she felt one tiny pea. Only a real princess could do that!"

So, without further ado, the prince married the princess, and the pea was placed in the royal museum, where it may be seen by one and all.

And now good night!

The Sleeping Beauty

Once upon a time, in a faraway land, there lived a king and queen who had no children. "Ah, if only we had a child!" they cried. But alas, they had none.

At long last a little girl was born. She was so beautiful that the king and queen could not contain their joy. They ordered a great feast to be prepared and invited all their relatives and friends. They also invited the fairies of the kingdom for good luck. Seven fairies received invitations, and seven golden plates were specially made for them to eat from.

There was, however, an eighth fairy in the land. As she was very old and no one had seen her for quite some time, she had been forgotten. When she appeared at the feast nonetheless, there was no golden plate for her. This made her very angry indeed.

On seeing the old one's wrath, a young fairy hid behind a curtain to watch what would happen.

When the feast ended, each fairy presented the royal child with a priceless gift. The first gave her beauty; the second, wisdom; the third, sweetness. The fourth fairy gave her a charming voice and the fifth, grace. The sixth fairy gave her a sense of humor.

Then the old fairy stood up and called out in a mean voice, "Here is my gift. In her fifteenth year the princess shall prick herself on a spindle and fall lifeless to the floor." Without another word, she turned and left the hall.

Everyone gasped, but the seventh fairy, whose wish was still unspoken, stepped from her hiding place. She could not lift the curse, but she could soften it. "The princess shall fall instead into a deep sleep lasting one hundred years," she said.

Determined to safeguard his dear child from this calamity, the king commanded that all spindles in the entire kingdom be burned.

As time went on every promise of the fairies came true. The princess grew up beautiful, wise, sweet, charming, graceful, and full of laughter. Everyone who met her loved her.

On the very day that the princess turned fifteen, however, it happened that the king and queen were away from the palace. For the first time, the princess was free to wander about the castle. In time, she came to an old tower. She went up its winding staircase and reached a door. Pushing it open, she found a little room where an old woman sat with a spindle.

"Good day," said the princess. "What are you doing?"

"I am spinning," the old woman said.

"What is the thing that whirls about?" asked the princess. As she reached for the spindle she pricked her finger.

72

Instantly, she fell into a deep sleep, and this same sleep descended on the entire castle.

When the king and the queen came home, they, too, fell asleep. All of their servants slept as well.

Around the castle a thick hedge of briar roses began to grow. Each year, for one hundred years, it grew higher and thicker, until at last it covered the whole castle. People living nearby told the story of the lovely Sleeping Beauty, as the king's daughter came to be called.

After a hundred years, a handsome prince came riding by and heard an old man tell of the castle that stood behind the briar hedge, and of the princess who lay asleep inside.

"I wish to look upon this Sleeping Beauty," the young prince said.

As luck would have it, this was the very day on which the princess was to wake. When the prince approached the briar hedge, its thick branches parted, making it easy for him to enter.

In the courtyard, nothing stirred. When he went into the castle, the king and queen lay sleeping by their thrones. Courtiers and servants slept nearby.

At last he reached the tower and the little room where Sleeping Beauty lay. She looked so beautiful that he could not take his eyes from her. He knelt down and gave her a kiss.

As his lips touched her cheek Sleeping Beauty opened her eyes and looked at him lovingly. Then, hand in hand, they went down from the tower.

The king and queen and all their courtiers, meanwhile, also woke up and looked at each other, astonished.

The prince and Sleeping Beauty were soon married, and their wedding was celebrated with much splendor. Needless to say, they lived happily every after.

The Wolf and the Seven Little Kids

Once upon a time, a mother goat had seven little kids whom she loved with all her heart. One spring morning she decided to go out into the field to gather tender green sprouts for her kids' supper. She picked up her basket and called the seven kids to her side.

"While I am gone," she said, "be sure to keep the door locked; open it for no one. Be especially careful of the clever wolf. He will try to fool you, but you can always recognize him by his rough voice and his black feet."

"Don't worry, dear Mother," bleated the kids. "We'll take care." So the mother goat went on her way with an easy mind.

Soon there came a knock at the door. A rough voice said, "Lift the latch, my dears. Mother is home and she's brought you each a present."

But the seven kids remembered what their mother had told them. "We will not open the door," they cried. "Our mother has a sweet voice. Yours is as rough as sandpaper. You are the wolf! Go away!"

So the crafty wolf ran to the grocer and bought a pot of honey. He licked it all up to make his voice sweet. Then he went back to the house of the seven little kids.

This time he knocked and said sweetly, "Lift the latch, my darlings. Mother is back with presents for you all." But the wolf had leaned a big black paw against the window, and the kids remembered what their mother had told them.

"We will not open the door," they cried. "Our mother has lovely white feet. Yours are black as coal. You are the wolf! Go away!"

Now the wolf ran straight to the baker. "Put white flour on my feet," he said, "or I will eat you up!" The frightened baker did as he was told, and the wolf walked with care back to the house of the seven little kids.

Gently he knocked, then sweetly said, "Lift the latch, my own dear goatlets. Mother is home at last, with presents for one and all."

"First show us your feet," said the cautious kids. The clever wolf held two flour-covered paws up to the window. Since the paws were white, the seven kids felt sure it was their mother. They lifted the latch and opened the door.

In bounded the wolf, and the little kids all ran to hide. One dived under the table; a second hid beneath the bedcovers; a third crouched behind the stove; a fourth squeezed under the sink, a fifth into the cupboard, and a sixth beside the washbowl. The youngest kid sprang into the clock case.

The wolf found them and gobbled them up, one right after the other—except for the smallest kid hiding in the clock case. Then, being quite full, the wolf went outside to take a nap.

When the mother goat came home, what a sight met her eyes! The house door was wide open; the furniture lay this way and that; the quilt had been ripped from the bed; and the washbowl lay broken to pieces. She looked for her dear children, but they were nowhere to be found. In tears, she called to them. There was no answer—except for the little voice of the youngest kid.

"I am in the clock case, dear Mother," he whispered. She took the frightened kid out and kissed him tenderly. He told her how the wolf had fooled them and had eaten all his brothers and sisters. The mother goat wept bitterly.

Unable to stay in the sad house a moment longer, she went outside. Then she heard the wolf snoring. Looking closely at the monster, she saw his fat belly moving. "Mercy me!" she said. "Can my poor children still be alive?"

She sent the littlest kid to fetch her scissors, a needle, and some thread. Then the mother goat cut open the cruel beast's stomach. No sooner had she made a small opening than one little kid's head popped out. She cut a bit more and all six kids leapt out, one after the other.

The little kids weren't hurt at all because the greedy wolf had swallowed them whole. What a joyous reunion they had with their mother!

Then the mother goat said, "Quickly, children. Find some big stones. We will put them in the wicked wolf's stomach while he is still asleep." This they did, and the mother goat sewed him up again.

When the wolf awoke, he felt thirsty. He stood up, which was not easy with all those rocks inside him, and walked to a nearby stream. As he bent over to drink, the heavy stones toppled the wolf right into the water, where he drowned.

The seven kids were watching and cried aloud, "The wicked wolf will bother us no more!" With their mother, they gathered in a circle, and all danced for joy.

The Town Mouse and the Country Mouse

Once upon a time, a country mouse invited his cousin, a town mouse, to visit him in the green meadow where he lived.

The Town Mouse came wearing an elegant suit and a beautiful polka-dot neckerchief. The Country Mouse set out the most elegant dinner he could offer: toasted barley seeds, kernels of fresh corn, vegetable roots, and pure spring water to drink. For dessert, there were wild blackberries.

But the Town Mouse didn't think much of this simple meal. After the two had eaten the last juicy berry, he turned to the Country Mouse and said, "Poor cousin! In this rustic place, you live no better than the ants or beetles. Come to town with me. I promise you will dine like a king."

So the Country Mouse agreed to go with the Town Mouse for a visit. The trip was long, and the cousins arrived after dark at a splendid house. It was brightly lit, as if by ten thousand fireflies.

Once inside, the Town Mouse led his cousin to a pantry filled with wondrous treats. On a wooden counter were tender bacon rinds, crumbs of rare cheeses, potato peelings, bits of soft butter, and several drops of wine in the bottoms of glasses.

The Country Mouse could scarcely believe his eyes. But no sooner had he begun to nibble than heavy footsteps approached. The pantry door swung open. "It's the cook!" whispered the Town Mouse. "Quick. Follow me." The cousins scampered off to hide in a small, uncomfortable hole.

When all was quiet, the Town Mouse took his frightened cousin back to the feast. The Country Mouse was about to swallow a tidbit of sponge cake when the pantry door opened again—this time slowly and softly. "Hah! The cat," said the Town Mouse, and the cousins scuttled for the safety of the cramped mouse hole.

At last the cat was gone, and the Town Mouse urged his cousin to finish his dinner. But the trembling Country Mouse had lost his appetite. He bade his cousin a hasty good-bye. "Your house is lovely and the food delectable," he said. "But, for me, I prefer to nibble my barley seeds and vegetable roots in the peace and quiet of a green meadow."

From that time on, though they exchanged Christmas and birthday cards, neither the Country Mouse nor the Town Mouse ever felt the need to visit each other again.